Little Teammate

Alan Williams

illustrated by Stephen Marchesi

NEW YORK

NASHVILLE   MELBOURNE

Little Teammate steps to the plate.
Just one hit will win this game.

Cheers get **louder.**

Pitcher looks **taller.**

Two strikes already and a runner on third...
Here comes the ball!

Crack! The bat sounds.

Surprise all over Little Teammate's face,
the ball flies over second base.

After the game,
a **big hug** from Daddy.

I **love** you Little Teammate.
I'm **proud** of you.
It makes me so **happy** to watch you play.

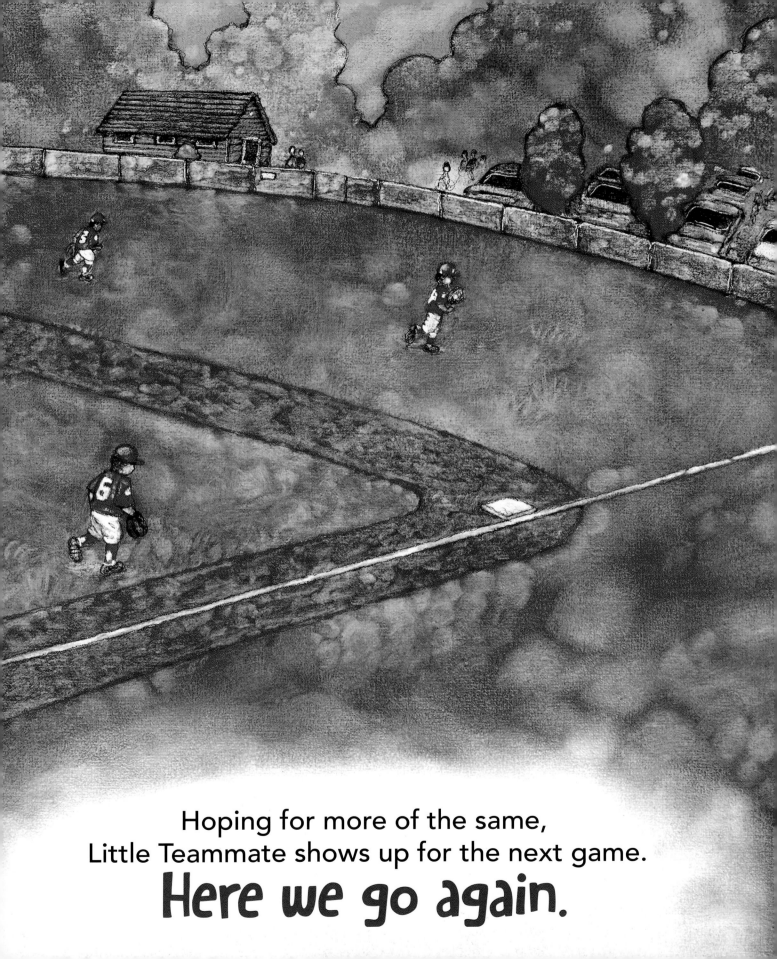

Hoping for more of the same,
Little Teammate shows up for the next game.
Here we go again.

Little Teammate steps to the plate.
Just one hit will win this game.

Cheers get **louder.**

Pitcher looks **taller.**

Two strikes already and a runner on third...
Here comes the ball!

Whiff! The bat makes no sound.

After the game,
a **big hug** from Daddy.

I **love** you Little Teammate.
I'm **proud** of you.
It makes me so **happy** to watch you play.

But Daddy...

You've said this before,
when my hit knocked
in the winning score.

Remember what you saw?
Today I missed that ball!

Yes Little Teammate,
but one thing
you must know...

I love you when you **hit** the ball.

I love you when you **miss** the ball.

I love you just because...

...because you are my Little Teammate.
And nothing can ever change that.

Daddy, I feel so much better!

For the next game I cannot wait...
What should I do when I step to the plate?

And always know that I'm your
biggest fan.

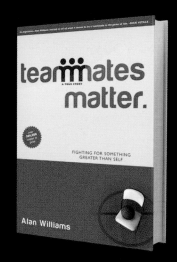
Little Teammate